To everyone that's got hair that wants to have
a little more fun than usual today,
Mamí and Papí,
the squad for always looking out,
and Tony

IMPRINT
A part of Macmillan Publishing Group, LLC
120 Broadway, New York, NY 10271

ABOUT THIS BOOK
The art for this book was created with Adobe Photoshop using Kyle T Webster's brushes and a Cintiq 13HD. The text was set
in Brandon Grotesque, and the display type is Mindset. The book was edited by Weslie Turner and designed by Carolyn Bull.
The production was supervised by Jie Yang, and the production editor was Hayley Jozwiak.

Printed in China by RR Donnelley Asia Printing Solutions Ltd., Dongguan City, Guangdong Province.

Library of Congress Cataloging-in-Publication Data is available.
ISBN 978-1-250-26177-9 (hardcover)

Our books may be purchased in bulk for promotional, educational, or business use. Please contact your local bookseller or the
Macmillan Corporate and Premium Sales Department at (800) 221-7945 ext. 5442 or by email at MacmillanSpecialMarkets@macmillan.com.

Imprint logo designed by Amanda Spielman
First edition, 2021

10 9 8 7 6 5 4 3 2 1
mackids.com

To one who steals this book today
Dare not and leave it be
For you'll be cursed with bad hair days,
A plight for all to see

STELLA'S
Stellar Hair

YESENIA MOISES

{Imprint}
MAKE YOUR MARK
NEW YORK

Stella didn't know *what* to do with her hair today.

IT TWISTED AND TURNED,
ZIGGED AND ZAGGED,
MADE LOOPITY-LOOPS AND LOTS OF CURLY Q'S.

It wasn't at all what she wanted.

"Momma! Momma!
My hair's not acting right!" Stella cried.

"Come here, baby—let me help you,"
Momma said.

"Uh-uh, Momma.
I want something special today—
it's the **BIG STAR LITTLE GALA!**"

"Well," Momma said, "maybe your auntie over on Mercury can give you a special style for your big day."

So Stella grabbed her hoverboard
and was on her way.

"What brings you to Mercury, honey?"
Aunt Ofelia said.

"Auntie, my hair's not acting right,"
Stella told her. "It twists and it turns
and it's not at all what I wanted!"

So Aunt Ofelia got to work on a **POOFY-SMOOTH STYLE.**

"So soft and elegant!" Stella said.
"Just like you! But I don't know if this is me."

"Then try visiting your auntie over on Venus!"
Aunt Ofelia said.

When Stella got to Venus,
Auntie Alma said, "Hey, girl, hey!"

"Auntie, Auntie!" Stella cried.
"My hair's not acting right. It zigs and
zags from poofy to straight!"

So Auntie Alma got to work
on a **ROYAL LION'S MANE**.

"So proud and fierce!" Stella exclaimed.
"Just like you. But it's all hair and no me!"

"Hmm . . . try seeing your auntie on Mars!"
Auntie Alma suggested.

Stella flew past Earth to
visit her third aunt.

"Welcome to Mars, dear!"
Aunt Rubi said.

"Auntie! My hair's not acting right!
It shifts and sways and
takes up all of my space!"

So Aunt Rubi got to work on an **ELEGANT CROWN** of hair.

"So strong and classy," Stella said softly.
"Just like you! But maybe too much for
someone like me?"

"See if your other aunts
can help you,"
Aunt Rubi replied.

On Jupiter, where everyone's hair appreciates a good storm, Auntie Cielo let the rain **SPLASH AND SPLOOSH** in Stella's hair.

Auntie Iris on Saturn gave her big
SPACE BUNS, wrapping her hair like rings
AROUND AND ROUND AND ROUND . . .

On Uranus, Stella's twin aunties got excited.

"Big, chunky **TWISTS!**"
Auntie Laila cried.

"No, **BRAIDS!**"
Auntie Lala argued.

So Stella ended up with braids and twists—
big and small—beads, shells, rings, and a big bun.

A hop skip away on Neptune,
Auntie Rio gave her **ENDLESS WAVES**.

"So deep and graceful," Stella whispered.
"Just like you. But I can't see me, and it's
almost time for the party."

And Auntie Rio said softly,
"Go see your auntie over by the Sun."

"Auntie Solana, my hair's
just not acting right," Stella said.

"It's been TWISTED AND TURNED

and TWIRLED AND SWIRLED

and SHIFTED AND SWAYED

and SPLISHED AND SPLOOSHED,

and it isn't at all what I wanted!"

"You know," Auntie Solana said, "there's really no such thing as hair not acting right—your hair just wants to be a little more fun today. And that's okay. You don't have to change a thing. **JUST BE YOURSELF.**"

So Stella washed her hair,
just like the rain on Jupiter did,
until it was oh so soft.

She put it up in two buns,
smaller than the ones
she had on Saturn.

She pulled it out into
a lion's mane,
as full as the ones on Venus.

She brushed it into Neptunian waves that snapped back into tight poofy Mercurial curls.

After a few braids and twists from Uranus, with a flair fit for Mars, she added something special from the Sun: warm stardust that glimmered with every step she took.

It was something new,
and not too different, but totally Stella!

IT TWISTED AND TURNED,

ZIGGED AND ZAGGED,

MADE LOOPITY-LOOPS AND LOTS OF CURLY Q'S . . .

. . . and that was perfectly
fine by her.

THE SUN is the center of our solar system—and way too hot to live on! If humans could live near the Sun, they might wear natural styles, like **DREADLOCKS**, worn in the hottest areas on Earth.

MERCURY is the planet closest to the Sun and turns so slowly that days are very long and hot—and nights are long and freezing cold! If humans could live on Mercury, they might wear styles that combine extreme opposites: half **AFRO PUFFS**, half **STRAIGHTENED HAIR**.

On **VENUS**, the atmosphere is dense and hot. Heat can make big hair even bigger, so if humans could live on Venus, they might just have the biggest **AFROS** the universe has ever seen!

Earth is the only planet where humans can actually breathe the air—and there are so many different types of human beings. It makes sense that Stella's style is **A LITTLE BIT OF EVERYTHING**.

The environment on **MARS** is harsh and dusty. If humans could live on Mars, they might wear protective styles like an **UPDO**. (Even so, Auntie's hair is red after years of living there!)

JUPITER's atmosphere is full of gas and giant storms. If humans could live on Jupiter, they might wear their hair in **NATURAL** styles. Hard to keep your hair in a fancy style when it's always raining!

SATURN is surrounded by a beautiful ring system made of ice. If humans could live on Saturn, they might wear their hair in **BUNS** and other round styles in honor of their planet's rings.

URANUS is a twin of the planet Neptune in almost every way— but it's the only planet that rotates as if tilted slightly sideways! If humans could live on Uranus, they might create topsy-turvy styles, like a mix of **TWISTS** and **BRAIDS**, to match the weirdness of their tilted planet.

NEPTUNE is the farthest planet from the Sun, with the coldest atmosphere. Scientists call the planet an "ice giant" or "water giant." (Uranus too!) If humans could live on Neptune, they might wear their hair **LONG AND WAVY**, in honor of their planet's watery surface and atmosphere.